NATASHA WING'S
The Night Before
Second Grade

Grosset & Dunlap

To second-grade teachers and students—NW

In loving memory of Donna DiGiacomo Schoen—AW

GROSSET & DUNLAP
An imprint of Penguin Random House LLC, New York

First published in the United States of America by Grosset & Dunlap,
an imprint of Penguin Random House LLC, New York, 2022

Text copyright © 2022 by Natasha Wing
Illustrations copyright © 2022 by Penguin Random House LLC

GROSSET & DUNLAP is a registered trademark of Penguin Random House LLC.

Visit us online at penguinrandomhouse.com.

Library of Congress Cataloging-in-Publication Data is available.

Printed in the United States of America

ISBN 9780593382745   10 9 8 7 6 5 4 3 2 1 COMM

NATASHA WING'S
The Night Before
Second Grade

By Natasha Wing
Illustrated by Amy Wummer

Grosset & Dunlap

'Twas the night before second grade,
I was out with my friend.
We couldn't believe summer vacation
had come to an end.

But we were so excited and ready for school,
even if it meant no more trips to the pool.

All through the summer, I read so many books
about castles, dinosaurs, and pirates with hooks!

But in second grade,
this is the first time
I'll read chapter books
and long poems in rhyme!

Jack thinks I'll have it
much too easy this year.
"Piece of cake," he said.
"You have nothing to fear!"

"I'm not sure," I told Jack. "I heard our teacher is tough.
Though I'm hoping he'll help us learn all kinds of new stuff."

Like inches and angles.

Addition!

Subtraction!

Multiplication
and even some fractions!

I can already count
from one to one hundred and back.

My dad always says I'm a real brainiac.

Mom had taken me shopping
for sneakers and jeans.
My legs have grown long—
like skinny string beans!

I picked out markers and notebooks,
plus a brand-new backpack.
Mom bought little boxes
of my favorite snack.

My backpack was hung
on a coat hook with care,
with my school spirit T-shirt
that I can't wait to wear.

That night I nestled
all snug in my bed,
while visions of chapter books
danced in my head.

"Time to go, you two!
Got everything, Nate?"

Dad was starting a new job
and he couldn't be late.

Mom dropped me off in front of the school.
Hey, look! All my friends are back together—how cool!

Each of us was wearing our school spirit T-shirts.
Check out our new shoes—we've all had growth spurts.

I was kind of nervous about going to class.
"It's going to be weird," I told my friend Cass.

Still, I couldn't wait to start the first day.
When the bell *brrringed*, I was on my way.

Where is our teacher?
I thought to myself.

Then in he came, as I put
all my stuff on my shelf.

When what to the class's amazed eyes should appear
but my dad in his school spirit T-shirt.
He was grinning, ear to ear.

"I'm your teacher," said Dad.
"You can call me Mr. Lee."

"Especially you," he joked,
pointing directly at me.

Dad let our class know
that even though I'm his son,
he won't play favorites.
He'll be fair to everyone.

I'm glad second grade is finally here. With Dad as my teacher, it'll be an interesting year!